Fireflies, Fireflies, Light My Way

Fireflies, Fireflies, Light My Way

By Jonathan London
Illustrated by Linda Messier

VIKING

Author's note

"Fireflies, fireflies, light my way" is a line from an old Mesaquakie lullaby, and was the inspiration for this book. The Mesaquakies, otherwise known as the People of the Red Earth, were a large and powerful tribe in the Great Lakes region during the seventeenth and eighteenth centuries. Now they live in a settlement along the Iowa River in Iowa.

It is to the Mesaquakie people that I give thanks for the use of these words.

VIKING
Published by the Penguin Group
Penguin Books USA Inc., 375 Hudson Street, New York, New York 10014, U.S.A.
Penguin Books Ltd, 27 Wrights Lane, London W8 5TZ, England
Penguin Books Australia Ltd, Ringwood, Victoria, Australia
Penguin Books Canada Ltd, 10 Alcorn Avenue, Toronto, Ontario, Canada M4V 3B2
Penguin Books (N.Z.) Ltd, 182-190 Wairau Road, Auckland 10, New Zealand

Penguin Books Ltd, Registered Offices: Harmondsworth, Middlesex, England

First published in 1996 by Viking, a division of Penguin Books USA Inc.

1 3 5 7 9 10 8 6 4 2

Text copyright © Jonathan London, 1996
Illustrations copyright © Linda Messier, 1996
All rights reserved

LIBRARY OF CONGRESS CATALOGING-IN-PUBLICATION DATA
London, Jonathan.
Fireflies, fireflies, light my way / by Jonathan London; illustrated by Linda Messier.   p.   cm.
Summary: A lively rhyming text that features fireflies, beavers, turtles and other
animals celebrates the interconnectedness of the natural world.
ISBN 0-670-85442-5
[1. Animals—Fiction. 2. Nature—Fiction. 3. Stories in rhyme.]
I. Messier, Linda, ill. II. Title.
PZ8.3.L8433Fi 1996 [E]—dc20   95-43203 CIP AC

Manufactured in China
Set in OptiFob

For Teri, Frank, Jean, Laurie, Marsha, Jane,
Melissa, et al.—a writers' group *extraordinaire!*
—J. L.

For Ma and Da
—L. M.

Fireflies, fireflies, light my way.

Lead me to the place . . .

. . . where the turtles play.
Turtles, turtles, dive so deep.

Lead me to the place . . .

. . . where the bullfrogs leap.
Bullfrogs, bullfrogs, leap away.

Lead me to the place . . .

. . . where the beavers play.
Beavers, beavers, gnaw on limbs.

Lead me to the place . . .

. . . where the catfish swims.
Catfish, catfish, swim your best.

Lead me to the place . . .

. . . where the wood ducks nest.

Wood ducks, wood ducks, squawk away.

Lead me to the place . . .

. . . where the muskrats play.
Muskrats, muskrats, paddle far.

Lead me to the place . . .

. . . where the raccoons are.
Raccoons, raccoons, sniff away.

Lead me to the place . . .

. . . where the crawdads stay.
Crawdads, crawdads, scuttle away.

Lead me to the place . . .

. . . where the otters play.
Otters, otters, slide some more.

Lead me to the place . . .

. . . *Yikes!* Where the alligators ROAR?
Alligators, alligators, give me a chance!

Chase me to the place . . .

. . . where the fireflies dance.
Fireflies, fireflies, light my way.

Lead me to the place . . .

. . . where the turtles dive

bullfrogs leap

beavers gnaw

catfish swim

wood ducks squawk

muskrats paddle

raccoons sniff

crawdads scuttle

otters slide . . .

. . . and no alligators chase me away!

Everybody, everybody, sing HURRAY!